Own Garden

Activities for Children 7 to 10 Years

Nicholle Carrière

LONE PINE

Contents

Gardening Is Fun 4
   Why Plant a Garden 4

Getting Started 6
   Before You Start 6
   Kinds of Gardens 8
   How to Begin 10
   Container Gardening 12

What You Need to Know 11
   Different Types of Plants 14
   What Is Dirt? 16
   How Do Seeds Grow? 18
   Pollination 20
   Making Compost 22

Let's Plant! 24
   Gardening Tools 24
   Planting Seeds 26
   Seed Packet Information 28
   Starting Seeds Indoors 30
   When to Plant 32
   Garden Safety 34

Caring for Your Garden 36
   Watering Your Garden 36
   Good Garden Bugs 38
   Bad Garden Bugs 40
   Weeds 42

In the Fall 44
Fall Cleanup 44

The Plants 46
Radishes 46
Beans 48
Carrots 50
Tomatoes 52
Peas 54
Beets 56
Strawberries 58
Zucchini 60
Cucumbers 62
Greens 64
Pumpkins 66
Peppers 68
Herbs 70
More Herbs 72
Onions 74
Potatoes 76
Sunflowers 78

Activities & Experiments 80
Watch Seeds Grow 80
Eggshell Garden 82
Rain Gauge 84
Garden Row Markers 86
A Garden Journal 88
Bug Hunt 90
Funny Plant Heads 92
Kitchen Scrap Garden 94

Why Plant a Garden?

Vegetables and fruits taste good, and they are good for you.

GARDENING IS FUN! • 5

Vegetables come in all the colors of the rainbow:

- Red—tomatoes, radishes, beets
- Orange—carrots, pumpkins
- Yellow—corn, yellow tomatoes, squash
- Green—lettuce, peas, beans, spinach
- Blue and Purple—purple cabbage, purple carrots, purple potatoes, eggplant
- White—onions, potatoes

GETTING STARTED

Before You Start

You need to think about many things before you begin planting your garden.

Where are you going to plant your garden:
- In the ground?
- In raised beds?
- In containers?

What size will your garden be? A big garden can be a lot of work, but you have room to grow more plants.

BEFORE YOU START • 7

If you don't have much space, you can grow plants in **containers** on your balcony or patio.

What do you want to plant? Do you have any favorite vegetables?

Plants like zucchini, potatoes and pumpkins need a lot of space. You can grow things like lettuce, beans, tomatoes and strawberries in smaller spaces.

8 • GETTING STARTED

Kinds of Gardens

In a **traditional garden**, you plant seeds right into the ground. This kind of garden can be small or very large.

Raised beds are wooden boxes filled with dirt. You can put raised beds wherever you like and make them any size or shape.

KINDS OF GARDENS • 9

Containers or pots work well if you don't have much space. This kind of garden is good for a balcony or patio. You can put just one plant in a container or plant a group of herbs or greens together.

A tabletop garden is a good way to garden for people who use a wheelchair or have mobility issues. You can grow plants in containers or make a special table with sections that hold soil.

10 • **GETTING STARTED**

How to Begin

Get an adult to help you measure your garden plot.

HOW TO BEGIN • 11

Write down how wide and how long the garden is. Then use the measurements on the seed packets to help plan the rows.

Draw a picture of your garden using lines for the rows.

Write the name or draw a picture of the vegetable you want to plant in each row.

Container Gardening

A **container garden** is good for small spaces. You can use a few large containers or groups of smaller pots.

Try planting groups of herbs together. If you plant greens like lettuce, spinach and kale in a big pot, you'll have a salad garden. Or try a pizza garden with tomatoes, basil and peppers!

CONTAINER GARDEN • 13

The soil in large containers stays moist longer, so you don't have to water them as often. Smaller pots dry out quickly and need to be watered daily.

Window boxes and hanging baskets work well for plants like strawberries, tomatoes and even cucumbers.

14 • **WHAT YOU NEED TO KNOW**

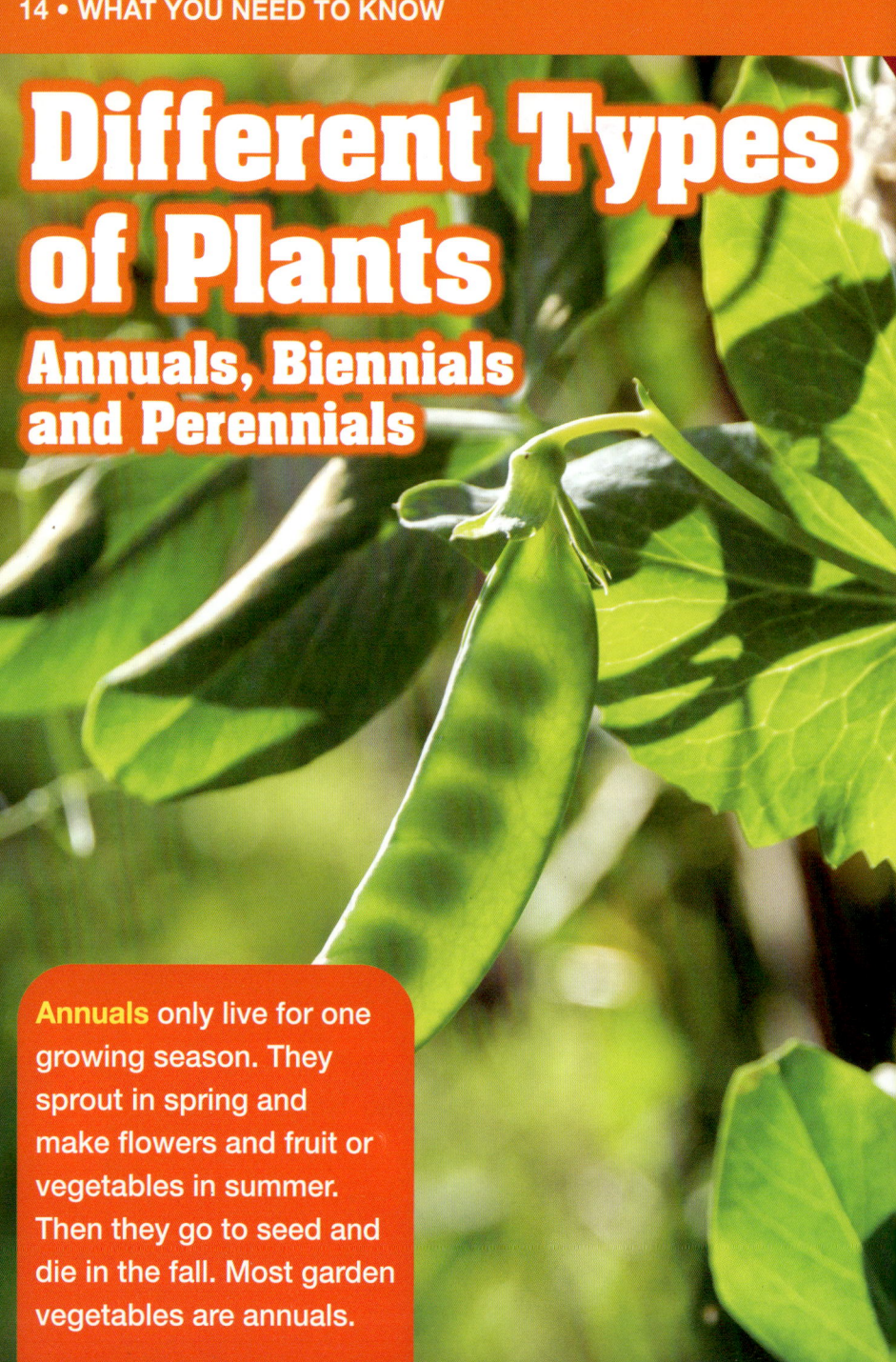

Different Types of Plants
Annuals, Biennials and Perennials

Annuals only live for one growing season. They sprout in spring and make flowers and fruit or vegetables in summer. Then they go to seed and die in the fall. Most garden vegetables are annuals.

DIFFERENT TYPES OF PLANTS • 15

Biennials grow for two seasons. Root vegetables like beets, carrots and onions are really biennials. If you don't pick them, the plants will grow new leaves and flowers the next spring!

Perennials live for more than two years. Every year, the plants grow leaves, flowers and then fruits or vegetables. The plants die in the fall and grow again the next spring! They can grow for many years. Strawberries, rhubarb and chives are common garden perennials.

16 • WHAT YOU NEED TO KNOW

What Is Dirt?

Another word for **dirt** is **soil**. Soil is made of four things.

1. Small rock pieces—sand, silt and clay—are all made of **minerals**. Some minerals dissolve in water, and the plants use them as food. Your body takes minerals from the plants you eat. It uses iron, calcium, magnesium and other minerals to keep you healthy.

WHAT IS DIRT? • 17

2. **Dead and living things.** When plants die, bacteria, fungi and other **microorganisms** (tiny living things) in the soil eat them. The microorganisms break down the dead stuff so plants can use it for food. Earthworms and other bugs in the soil do the same thing.

3. Soil has a lot of **empty spaces filled with air.** Plant roots need air to live.

4. **Water** fills some of the spaces in soil. Plant roots need water. Without water, the plants die. Water is important to keep plants alive and growing.

18 • WHAT YOU NEED TO KNOW

How Do Seeds Grow?

Seeds need four things to grow: **water, air, sun and warmth**. When a seed has these things, it starts to **sprout** or **germinate**. The roots grow first. They grow out of the seed and down into the soil.

Next, a little plant called a **seedling** pushes its way out of the soil. As it grows, it gets food from the soil.

HOW DO SEEDS GROW? • 19

The plant's leaves use sunlight, water and air to make food for the plant. This is called **photosynthesis**.

When the plant is big enough, it makes flowers. The flowers become vegetables and fruits like beans, peas, strawberries, zucchinis and cucumbers.

Vegetables like beets, carrots and potatoes grow from plant roots.

What do plants drink?
Root beer.

Pollination

The bright colors and scent of flowers attracts bees. They like to eat the sweet nectar that the flowers make. They also use the nectar to make honey.

Inside the flower is a yellow powder called **pollen**. When a bee is collecting nectar, some of the pollen gets stuck to the bee.

When the bee visits other flowers, the pollen gets brushed off. It falls inside the flower and enters egg cells. This is called **pollination**. When a flower is pollinated, it can make fruit (or vegetables) and seeds.

POLLINATION • 21

Other insects such as butterflies, flies, moths and wasps also pollinate flowers. so do bats, birds and the wind.

Without bees, butterflies and other creatures to pollinate flowers, we wouldn't have any vegetables or fruit to eat. **Pollinators are important!**

22 • WHAT YOU NEED TO KNOW

Making Compost

Compost is plant food! It helps plants grow bigger and stronger.

Compost looks a lot like soil. It is made of organic matter like grass clippings, fruit and vegetable scraps, eggshells, coffee grounds and dead leaves. **Microorganisms** (tiny microscopic creatures) break down all the plant material. It's like recycling!

To make compost, you need a bin or pile that is about 3 feet (1 meter) high, 3 feet (1 meter) wide and 3 feet (1 meter) deep. Add any kind of plant matter to the compost bin, except weeds.

MAKING COMPOST • 23

Water the compost pile from time to time. Use a shovel or garden fork to turn the compost over or poke holes in it. The microorganisms need air to work!

It takes time for the microorganisms to make **compost**. If you start a compost pile in the spring, it will be ready to use in the fall or next spring.

Gardening Tools

Here are some tools and other things you will need for gardening.

Shovel

Rake

Hoe

Trowel

GARDENING TOOLS • 25

Garden claw

Garden fork

Tape measure

Scissors
String

Watering can

What kind of table can you eat?
A vegetable

Planting Seeds

How do you know how far apart to plant seeds? Or how deep? Or how far apart the rows should be?

Look at the back of the seed packets. The information there will tell you how far apart and how deep to plant the seeds. It will also say how far apart the rows should be and how long the seeds take to **germinate**.

PLANTING SEEDS • 27

To make straight rows, use two sticks joined with a piece of string. Put a stick into the ground on each side of the garden with the string stretched in between. Then it's easy to make a straight row between the sticks.

What kind of vegetables do they grow in Antarctica?

Frozen ones

Seed Packet Information

Everything you need to know about planting seeds is on the back of the seed packet.

SEED PACKET INFORMATION

- How long the seeds take to sprout
- How deep to plant the seeds
- How far apart to plant the seeds
- How far apart to put the plants (if you started them indoors)
- How far apart the rows should be
- A description of the plant (this is a seed packet for chives)
- Suggestions for fertilizing

Days to Sprout	Seed Depth	Seed Spacing	Plant Spacing	Row Spacing
7-14	1.3 cm (1/2")	2.5 cm (1")	15 cm (6")	30 cm (12")
Jours à Germination	Profondeur de semence	Distance des semences	Distance des plants	Espacement de rangée

Chives form clumps of grass-like hollow leaves with a mild onion flavor. Develops attractive lavender-pink flowers. Delicious in soups, salads, cheese, egg dishes and with sour cream on baked potatoes. Can be grown indoors. Clumps may be divided and transplanted in spring after first season. Harvest often by cutting 5 cm (2") from the ground. Can be dried or frozen. Perennial. Zone 3

Fertilize with natural resources such as compost or manure. No herbicides, pesticides or man made fertilizers were used in the production of these seeds.

La ciboulette forme des touffes de feuilles en forme de graminée, creuses à saveur légère d'oignon. Ses jolies fleurs sont rose lavande. Délicieuse dans la soupe, la salade, avec les mets à base de fromage ou d'oeufs et aussi, bien sûr, sur les pommes de terre au four avec de la crème sure. Peut être planté à l'intérieur. On peut diviser et repiquer ses touffes au printemps à près une première saison de croissance. Récoltez souvent en coupant les feuilles à 5 cm (2") du sol. Peut être séchée ou congelée. Vivace. Zone 3

Fertilisez avec des ressources naturelles telles que le compost ou le fumier. Aucun herbicide, pesticide ou engrais artificiel ont été utilisés dans la production de ces semences.

7 78054 00045 0

30 • LET'S PLANT!

Starting Seeds Indoors

Many seeds, like carrots, beets and beans, can be planted right into the soil. Other seeds, like tomatoes, cucumbers and peppers, need to be planted indoors to sprout and grow for a few weeks. Then you can put the little plants into the garden when the weather is warm enough.

STARTING SEEDS INDOORS • 31

To start your seeds, you need small pots and potting soil. You can even use egg cartons or yogurt containers. Fill the containers with soil but leave a bit of room at the top.

Now plant the seeds! Cover the seeds with soil and gently water the containers. Put the containers in a warm, sunny spot.

You can also buy small plants at a garden center. These are called **bedding plants**.

When to Plant

When you plant your garden depends on where you live. If you plant seeds outside when it is too cold, they won't grow well. If you plant them too late, the vegetables may not have time to finish growing before it gets cold.

Find out the date of the **last frost** in the spring for your area and the date of the **first frost** in the fall. The time between the last spring frost and the first fall frost is the **growing season**. You can find this information online or at a garden center.

WHEN TO PLANT • 33

Make a list of the seeds you want to plant. The seed packets will tell you how long the vegetables take to grow. Plants that take longer to grow, like tomatoes, peppers and cucumbers, should be started indoors a few weeks before you want to plant them outside.

Garden Safety

Wear closed-toed shoes or rubber boots.

Make sure you have sunscreen, sunglasses and a hat.

Don't run with tools. When using sharp tools, keep the sharp part below your waist and point it at the ground.

GARDEN SAFETY • 35

Don't leave tools where people can step on or trip over them. When you are finished using garden tools, brush off the dirt and put them away.

Always wash your hands after gardening.

36 • CARING FOR YOUR GARDEN

Watering Your Garden

Water your garden once or twice a week. Plants grow best when you water them regularly but letting them dry out a bit helps the roots grow stronger.

WATERING YOUR GARDEN • 37

Water early in the morning or in the evening. If you water in the middle of the day when it's hot, a lot of the water just **evaporates** into the air.

Plants drink water through their roots. Use enough water so that it soaks down into the soil to reach the roots. Use a stick or trowel to dig down a bit to check.

Good Garden Bugs

Ladybug larvae

Ladybugs and **lacewings** eat aphids, bug eggs and larvae (young bugs). Their larvae, which don't look at all like the adults, also eat aphids, bug eggs and other pests that chew up the leaves of your garden plants.

Lacewing

GOOD GARDEN BUGS • 39

When **bees** visit flowers for nectar to make honey, they also collect pollen. They pollinate the flowers, helping them make the vegetables we love.

Butterflies also help pollinate flowers. And they're pretty to look at!

Earthworms make tunnels in the soil. This brings air to the plant roots. Earthworm poop is also good food for plants!

40 • CARING FOR YOUR GARDEN

Bad Garden Bugs

Many bugs and other creatures enjoy eating the leaves and vegetables of garden plants. The best way to get rid of these is to pick them off by hand. Yes, really!

Slug

Slugs look like snails without shells. They eat lettuce, spinach and other greens. They leave gooey slime trails as they move.

BAD GARDEN BUGS • 41

Aphids

Aphids are tiny green bugs. They suck the juice out of stems and leaves. They leave behind a sticky juice called **honeydew**. Aphids are a favorite food of ladybugs and lacewings.

Cutworm

Cutworms are fat worms about 1 inch (2.5 cm) long. They live in the soil and mostly come out at night. Cutworms chew through the stems of plants. Sometimes they eat the whole plant!

What do you call a homeless snail?

A slug

Weeds

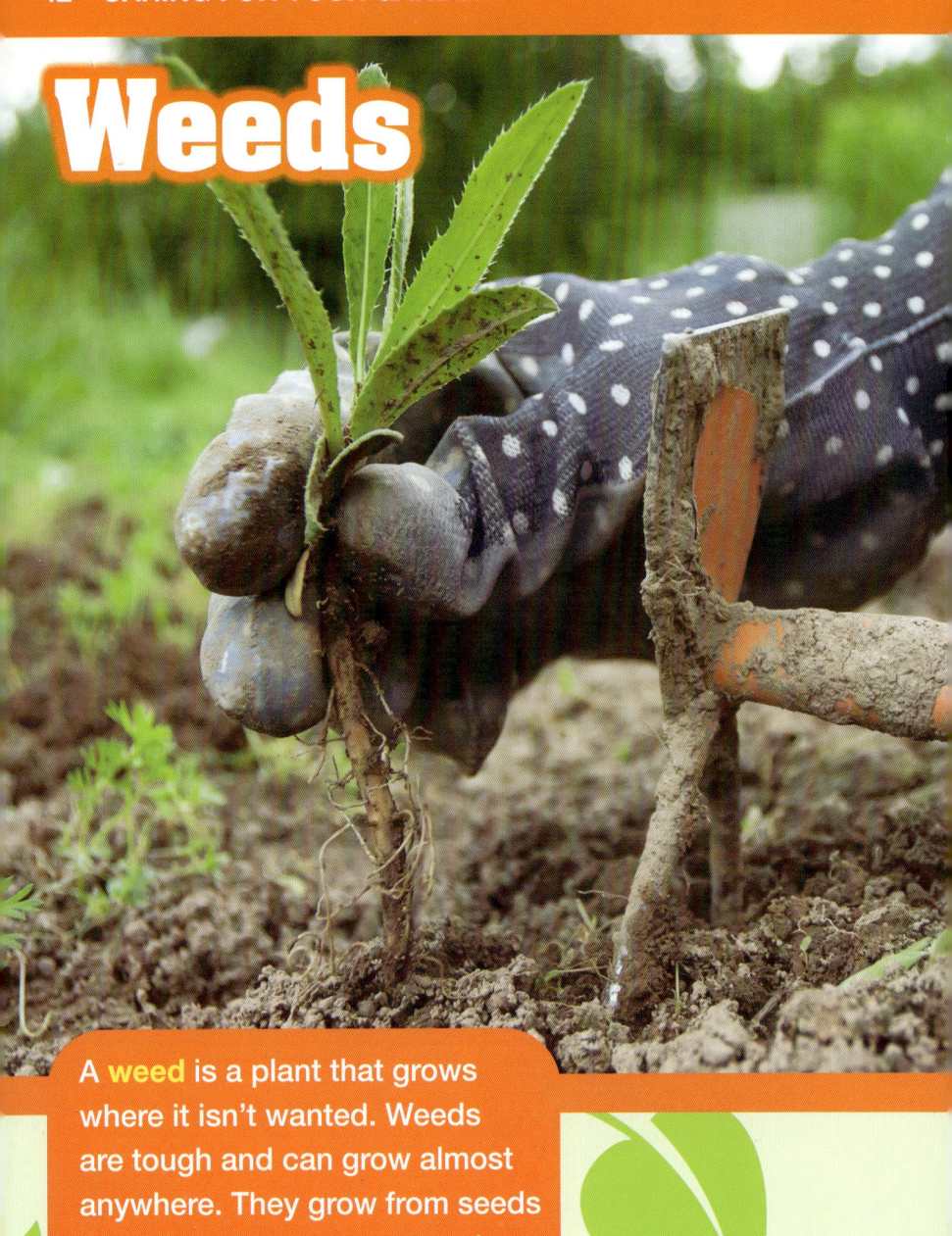

42 • CARING FOR YOUR GARDEN

A **weed** is a plant that grows where it isn't wanted. Weeds are tough and can grow almost anywhere. They grow from seeds that are blown into your garden by the wind or brought by birds or bugs.

WEEDS • 43

Weeds **rob** your plants by stealing food and water from the soil. They take up space and make shade that keeps the garden plants from growing well.

The best way to get rid of weeds is to pull them out by hand. Be sure to get all the roots, or the weeds will just grow back. You can use a trowel to loosen the soil and make it easier to pull the weeds out.

Fall Cleanup

In the fall, after you pick all your vegetables, it's time to **put your garden to bed**.

Start by cleaning up the dead plants and pulling out all the weeds. You can add the plants to the compost pile, but not the weeds.

FALL CLEANUP • 45

You can dig the dead vegetable plants, grass clippings and fallen leaves into the soil. They will break down over the winter and become food for future plants.

Make sure to clean off your garden tools and put them away so they will be ready and waiting for gardening next spring!

Radishes

Radishes have a spicy flavor. They grow fast, and the first plants appear three to seven days after planting. They are ready to eat in about 30 days.

You can eat the whole radish plant, not just the root. Be careful, though, because the leaves are bitter!

RADISHES • 47

If the plants look crowded, you can thin them by pulling out the littlest ones. That way, the others will have more room to grow, and the radishes will get bigger!

Most radishes are round, but some are long and skinny. Besides the usual red color, radishes can be white, black, yellow and watermelon (green on the outside and red on the inside).

Beans

Beans are easy to plant because the seeds are so big. They grow quickly, and you can pick them after about 45 days.

Bush beans grow to be about 1 foot (30 cm) tall. You can eat the long, green pods either raw or cooked. Some bean plants have yellow or purple pods.

BEANS • 49

Runner or pole beans grow on long vines. They need the support of a pole, trellis or fence. You can even grow them around a structure like a teepee or tunnel and make your own hideaway.

What's the fastest vegetable?

A runner bean

// THE PLANTS

Carrots

Pulling carrots out of the ground is fun. If you give them a quick wash, you can eat them right away. **Carrots** are usually orange, but they can also be red, yellow and even purple!

CARROTS • 51

Carrot seeds are very small, so it's easy to plant them too close together. When the leaves start to grow, you can **thin** them by pulling out the littlest carrots so the others have more room.

Carrots are biennials, meaning they have a **two-year life cycle**. If you leave a carrot in the ground over the winter, the next spring, the top will grow flowers and then go to seed.

The heaviest carrot weighed 20.4 pounds (10.17 kg), about the same as two big bags of potatoes. The longest carrot measured 20.5 feet (6.2 m), which is probably as long as your living room.

Tomatoes

Tomatoes are some of the most popular garden plants. You can grow little cherry tomatoes, regular-sized tomatoes like the ones you see in the supermarket or giant beefsteak tomatoes.

Tomatoes can be red, yellow, purple or even striped!

TOMATOES • 53

Start tomato seeds indoors in trays or small pots about 6 to 8 weeks before you want to plant them in the garden. Put them in a warm, sunny spot when the soil has warmed up. You can also buy tomato plants at garden centers.

The heaviest tomato weighed 9.65 pounds (4.38 kg). That's about the same as a cat or small dog.

What did the father tomato say to the baby tomato while on a family walk?

"Ketchup!"

54 • THE PLANTS

Peas

There are two kinds of **peas**. Regular **garden peas** have tough outer pods that you open to get the round, tasty peas inside. **Snow peas** have flat pods, and you can eat the whole thing pod and all!

PEAS • 55

Most peas grow on vines, so they need a fence or trellis for support. You can plant two rows of peas and put the trellis in the middle so the pea vines can grow up both sides.

You can cook peas, but the best way to eat them is straight out of the garden!

What do you call an angry pea?

Grum-pea

56 • THE PLANTS

Beets

Beets are a root vegetable, but you can eat the leaves, too! They taste a bit like spinach when cooked.

The seeds take about 14 days to germinate. Once the leaves start to grow, you can pull out the littlest plants to give the others room to get bigger.

BEETS • 57

Sometimes when you eat beets, your pee turns pink! Don't worry. It goes away in a day or two.

Beets are usually purplish-red, but they can also be orange, yellow, white and striped.

The heaviest beet weighed 53 pounds (24 kg), which is probably as heavy as the mattress on your bed.

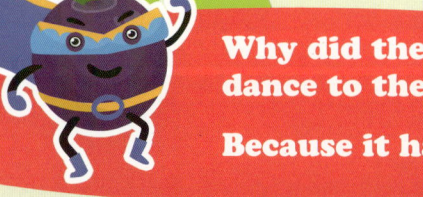

Why did the people dance to the vegetable band?

Because it had a good beet.

58 • THE PLANTS

Strawberries

Most garden plants are vegetables, but **strawberries** are a kind of fruit. They're easy to grow and taste really good, so they make a great addition to your garden.

STRAWBERRIES • 59

Buy strawberry plants from the garden center. There are different kinds, but they all like to grow in warm, sunny places.

Plant strawberries about 12 inches (30 cm) to 15 inches (45 cm) apart.

Strawberries are perennials, which means you don't have to plant them every year. They grow back in the spring.

60 • THE PLANTS

Zucchini

To plant **zucchini** seeds, make little **hills** about 2 feet (60 cm) apart. Put two or three seeds in each hill. Don't plant them too early in the spring. Zucchini seeds like warm soil.

Zucchinis taste best when they are young and tender. Watch them carefully! Once they start to grow, they can grow more than 1 inch (2.5 cm) every day!

ZUCCHINI • 61

Yellow squash is related to zucchini, and you plant it the same way. It also tastes the same.

What kind of vegetable likes to look at animals?

A zoo-chini

Cucumbers

Start growing **cucumber** plants from seed indoors 2 to 4 weeks before you want to plant them outside. You can also buy cucumber plants from a garden center. Make sure you put them in a sunny spot. Cucumbers like it warm! They also like lots of water!

CUCUMBERS • 63

There are two kinds of cucumbers. **Slicing cucumbers** are long and smooth. **Pickling cucumbers** are short and kind of prickly.

Cucumbers are good in sandwiches and salads, but they also taste great right out of the garden!

What's the most uncomfortable vegetable?

Spin-ouch!

Greens

Everyone knows that **leafy greens** are good for you! They grow well in the shady parts of your garden.

Lettuce can be red, purple or green. Some kinds grow in heads, a tight group of leaves that you pick all at once. Other kinds can be picked by the leaf all through the growing season.

Spinach grows quickly. You can pick it when the leaves are about 6 inches (15 cm) long, and the plant has about 8 leaves. If you just pick some of the outer leaves, the plant will keep growing.

GREENS • 65

Chard is related to beets. The stems are bright colors like yellow, pink, red, orange, purple, white and green. Cut the older leaves from each plant to cook and eat, and leave the others to keep growing.

Kale is one of the most nutritious vegetables. Most kinds have curly leaves, but dinosaur kale has long, bumpy leaves. National Kale Day is October 5!

What did the salad say to the dressing?

Lettuce be friends!

Pumpkins

You can grow your own Halloween **pumpkins!** Some kinds of pumpkins are small, but others grow to be really big. The biggest one weighed 2624.6 pounds (1190.5 kg). That's as heavy as a small car!

PUMPKINS • 67

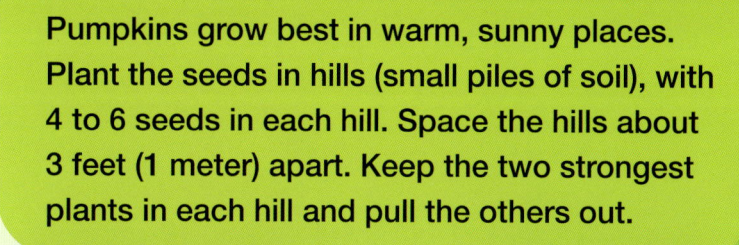

Pumpkins grow best in warm, sunny places. Plant the seeds in hills (small piles of soil), with 4 to 6 seeds in each hill. Space the hills about 3 feet (1 meter) apart. Keep the two strongest plants in each hill and pull the others out.

Remember that pumpkins aren't just for Jack-o'-lanterns. You can toast and eat the seeds or make pumpkin pie from the pulp.

How do you fix a cracked pumpkin?

With a pumpkin patch

68 • THE PLANTS

Peppers

Peppers come in all shapes, sizes and colors. They can be either sweet or hot. Some of the smallest peppers are the hottest!

Start pepper seeds indoors about 8 to 10 weeks before planting them in the garden. You can also buy pepper plants in garden centers. They often have many different kinds to choose from.

Peppers grow best in hot, sunny places. They are green when young and change color as they ripen.

The hottest pepper in the world is called **dragon's breath.** It's so hot that it isn't safe to eat!

Herbs

Dill is used to make dill pickles and flavor other foods! It can grow 5 feet (1.5 meters) tall. The dill flavor comes from the feathery leaves.

Basil has a strong smell and a strong flavor. The leaves are often used in Italian dishes like tomato sauce and pizza. Buy basil plants at a garden center and plant them in a hot, sunny spot.

HERBS • 71

Chives are related to onions. You eat the leaves, which are narrow tubes with pointy ends. You can also eat the flowers. They taste like onions, too! Chives are perennials, so they grow back every spring.

Mint is easy to grow. The most common kinds are peppermint and spearmint, but you can also try orange, ginger and chocolate mint. This herb spreads quickly and can take over the garden, so you might want to grow it in a pot.

What do you call a cheerleading herb?

An encourage mint!

72 • THE PLANTS

More Herbs

Parsley has a bitter flavor but lots of vitamins! It is related to carrots. Parsley leaves and carrot leaves taste kind of the same. Some kinds of parsley have curly leaves and other kinds have flat leaves.

MORE HERBS • 73

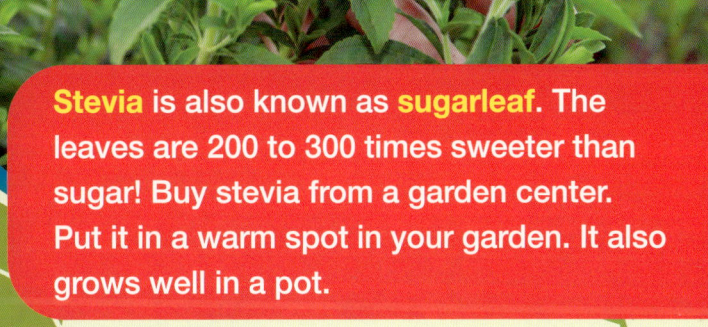

Stevia is also known as **sugarleaf**. The leaves are 200 to 300 times sweeter than sugar! Buy stevia from a garden center. Put it in a warm spot in your garden. It also grows well in a pot.

Catnip is in the mint family. Cats really like the strong scent. Humans can eat it, too. You can use the dried leaves to make tea. Be careful where you plant it because all the neighborhood cats will come to visit!

Why do mushrooms get invited to all the parties?

Because they are such fungis (Fun guys, get it?)

Onions

An **onion** is really a kind of root called a **bulb**.

You grow big onions by planting little onion seedlings or **sets** (small bulbs) that you buy at a garden center. Plant the sets in a sunny spot. Space them 4 to 5 inches (10 to 12 cm) apart.

ONIONS • 75

Onions can be white, yellow or purplish-red. The flavor varies from mild to strong. You can eat both the bulbs and the green tops.

Cutting onions releases a chemical called **allyl**. It's what makes you cry.

What kind of jewelry do vegetables wear?

Onion rings

76 • THE PLANTS

Potatoes

Potatoes can be brown, yellow, red or purple. The inside can be white, yellow, pink or purple. They are **tubers,** which is a kind of root.

To get big potatoes, you plant little **seed potatoes.** You can also cut up a large potato into pieces with one or two **eyes** per piece and plant those.

POTATOES • 77

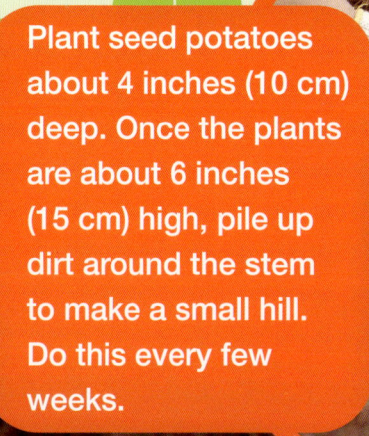

Plant seed potatoes about 4 inches (10 cm) deep. Once the plants are about 6 inches (15 cm) high, pile up dirt around the stem to make a small hill. Do this every few weeks.

You can dig up the potatoes once the tops of the plants start to die. Use a garden fork or shovel. Be careful not to cut or bruise them!

What vegetable has eyes but can't see?

A potato

Sunflowers

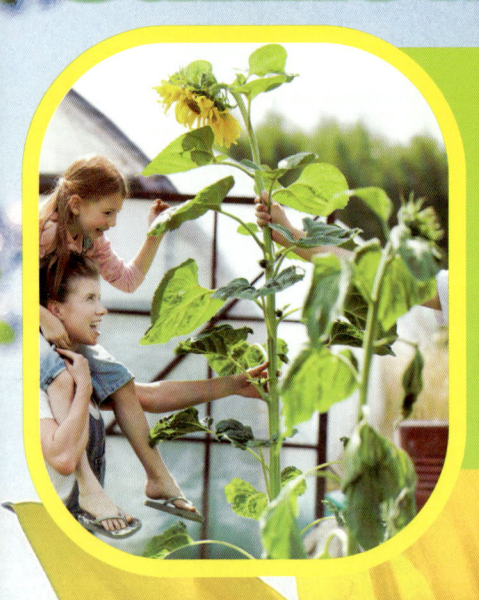

Sunflowers are the tallest garden plants, though some grow just a few feet tall. The biggest sunflower ever grown was more than 30 feet (9 meters) tall. That's taller than a giraffe!

Sunflowers can be white, yellow or orange. The seeds grow in the middle part of the flower. Birds love to eat them, and so do people!

SUNFLOWERS • 79

Pick the sunflower heads when the heads droop, and the seeds fall out easily.

Young sunflowers always turn to face the sun. They face east in the morning and follow the sun, so they face west at the end of the day. During the night, they turn to face east again.

80 • ACTIVITIES & EXPERIMENTS

Watch Seeds Grow

MATERIALS
Clear plastic cups
Paper towels or potting soil
Bean seeds
Water

Watch seeds grow by planting them in a clear cup!

Crumple up some paper towels and put them in the cup. Add some water so the paper towels are wet all the way through.

If you're using potting soil, fill the cups but leave some space at the top. Then water the soil so it is moist.

WATCH SEEDS GROW • 81

Choose three or four bean seeds. Make sure they aren't split. Put them into the cup between the side of the cup and the paper towels or soil so you can see them.

Put the cup in a sunny spot and watch the seeds grow! You'll see the roots sprout first and then the stem.

ACTIVITIES & EXPERIMENTS

Eggshell Garden

MATERIALS
- Eggs
- Egg carton
- Potting soil
- Seeds

You can start plants indoors using eggshells and an egg carton.

First crack the eggs and rinse out the shells. You might want to ask an adult to save up some eggshells for this activity.

Put the shells in the egg carton. Use a spoon to fill the shells with potting soil. Plant a couple of seeds in each one.

EGGSHELL GARDEN • 83

Water the eggshells just enough so the soil is moist all the way through. Don't make them too wet.

Put the carton in a sunny place. The plants should start to grow in about a week. Be sure to keep the soil moist. Don't let it dry out!

84 • ACTIVITIES & EXPERIMENTS

Rain Gauge

MATERIALS
Wide-mouth jar
Plastic ruler
Paper and pencil
Tape

How much rain does your garden get? Find out by making a rain gauge!

- Put the ruler in the jar with the numbers facing out.
- The number "1" should be at the bottom.
- Tape the ruler in place so it doesn't move.

Take the jar outside and put it somewhere out in the open (not under any trees). Try to put it somewhere where no one will kick it over. You can also put it on a fence post.

RAIN GAUGE • 85

After it rains, go outside and look at the ruler to see how much water is in the jar. Write down the amount. Then pour out the water and wait until it rains again!

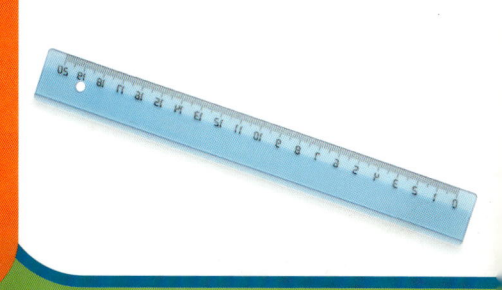

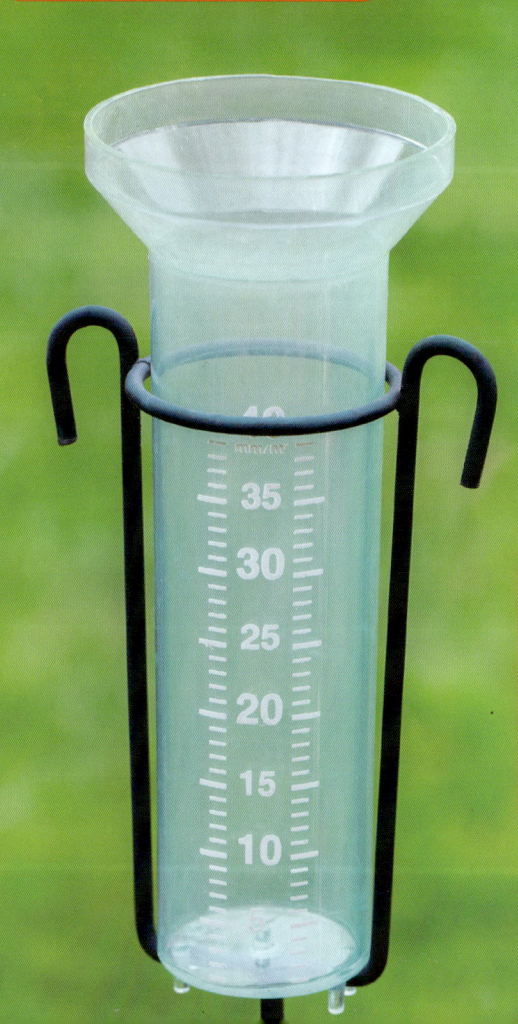

You can keep track of how much rain falls during each storm. You can also add up the amounts for each week or month.

86 • ACTIVITIES & EXPERIMENTS

Garden Row Markers

MATERIALS
Colored craft sticks
Felt markers

How do remember which plants are in each row of your garden? Make some colorful row markers!

Decide which colors you want to use. You can use a different color for each vegetable.

GARDEN ROW MARKERS • 87

Write the names of the vegetables on the sticks with the markers. Put the sticks at the ends of the rows in the garden and watch the plants grow!

88 • ACTIVITIES & EXPERIMENTS

A Garden Journal

MATERIALS

Notebook

Pen or pencil

Crayons or colored pencils

It's fun to keep track of how your garden is growing. You can write down which plants grew the best and how long they took to grow. You can even keep track of the weather!

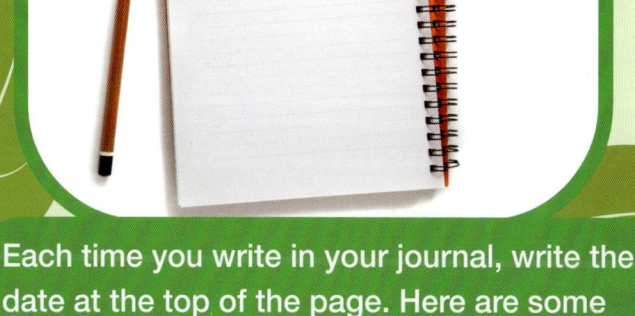

A GARDEN JOURNAL • 89

Each time you write in your journal, write the date at the top of the page. Here are some things you might want to write down:
- What day you planted your seeds
- How long the seeds took to sprout. Which seeds came up first?
- The weather: Is it sunny, cloudy, raining? What's the temperature?
- What days you watered the garden
- Did you see any interesting bugs? Butterflies? Caterpillars?
- What day did you pick your vegetables?

Journals don't have to be just words. You can use crayons or colored pencils to draw pictures of the plants or bugs in your garden. Use your imagination!

90 • ACTIVITIES & EXPERIMENTS

Bug Hunt

MATERIALS

Magnifying glass

**Paper and pencil
(or your garden journal)**

Camera or phone (optional)

Gardens are full of life! Be a detective and take a closer look at the creatures in yours!

Start by looking for flying bugs like **butterflies, bees and dragonflies**. How many can you find? Watch how they fly. Do they like to land on certain kinds of plants?

Take a closer look at the plants. Use your magnifying glass. What can you see in the soil?

Are there any bugs on or under the leaves? Are they eating the plants?

What time of day do you see the most bugs? What's the biggest bug you saw? What's the most interesting? Do you have a favorite bug?

92 • ACTIVITIES & EXPERIMENTS

Funny Plant Heads

MATERIALS

- Old pair of pantyhose
- Potting soil
- Grass or chive seeds
- Pipe cleaners, googly eyes, little pompoms or other craft supplies
- Rubber bands
- Craft glue or glue gun
- Shallow dish

FUNNY PLANT HEADS • 93

You can make heads with funny faces and grassy hair.

- Cut a tube about 6 to 8 inches (15 to 20 cm) long from the pantyhose.
- Tie a knot in one end.
- Turn the tube inside out. It will look like a little bag.

- Put a few teaspoons of seeds in the bag.
- Fill the rest of it with potting soil and tie the end closed.
- Use your hands to shape it to look like a round head. If you want, you can twist parts of the bag to make ears and a nose.
- Use rubber bands to hold them in place.

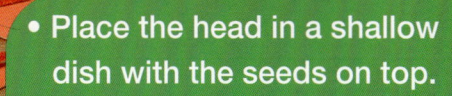

- Place the head in a shallow dish with the seeds on top.
- Use the craft supplies and glue to make a face.

- After the glue is dry, carefully water your head and put it in a warm place. The seeds should start to grow in a few days.
- Once the hair has grown, you can give it a haircut or hairstyle.

94 • ACTIVITIES & EXPERIMENTS

Kitchen Scrap Garden

MATERIALS
Vegetable scraps
Containers
Potting soil

You can grow an indoor garden from vegetable scraps!

- Cut the tops off carrots and beets and put them in containers filled with soil.
- Put them in a sunny spot and keep the soil moist.
- The scraps should start to sprout in a week or so.

KITCHEN SCRAP GARDEN

You can also try garlic cloves, the bottoms (white part) of green onions or the bottom of a bunch of celery.

You can also grow potatoes. Cut off the eyes of a potato, leaving some of the potato attached. Plant the eyes in a container with soil. Water them and watch them grow!

© 2021 by Lone Pine Media Productions (B.C.) Ltd.
Printed in China

All rights reserved. No part of this work covered by the copyrights hereon may be reproduced or used in any form or by any means—graphic, electronic or mechanical—or stored in a retrieval system or transmitted in any form by any means without the prior written permission of the publisher, except for reviewers, who may quote brief passages. Any request for photocopying, recording, taping or storage on information retrieval systems of any part of this work shall be directed in writing to the publisher.

Distributed by: Canada Book Distributors - Booklogic
www.canadabookdistributors.com
www.lonepinepublishing.com
Tel: 1-800-661-9017

Library and Archives Canada Cataloguing in Publication
Title: My very own garden : activities for children 7 to 10 years / Nicholle Carrière.
Names: Carrière, Nicholle, 1961– author.
Identifiers: Canadiana (print) 2021011486X | Canadiana (ebook) 20210115025 | ISBN 9781774510100 (softcover) | ISBN 9781774510124 (PDF)
Subjects: LCSH: Gardening—Juvenile literature. | LCSH: Plants—Juvenile literature.
Classification: LCC SB457 .C37 2021 | DDC j635—dc23

Cover Images: Front cover: From GettyImages: Yana Tatevosian.
Back cover: From GettyImages: travnikovstudio, Zaikina, AwesomeShotz.
Backgrounds: From GettyImages: MrsWilkins
Cartoon vegetables: From GettyImages: Tetiana Lazunova; VikiVector; the8monkey; luplupme
Cartoon bugs: From GettyImages: worldofvector

Photo credits: Nicholle Carriere, 29. From GettyImages: 1181357162, 9; 1550539, 25; 815474792, 24; Ailime, 71; Akchamczuk, 41, 47, 54, 73; Akintevs, 14; Oksana Aksenova, 9; Alexander62, 53; Mehriban Aliyeva, 95; AND-ONE, 34; andrewburgess, 24; Anest, 18; annalovisa, 23; Abdulkadir ARSLAN, 77; ArtesiaWells, 35; Asergieiev, 84; AtomStudios, 18; AVNphotolab, 59; AwesomeShotz, 83; BasieB, 49; Ben-Schonewille, 85; Laurence Berger, 62; Black_Kira, 86; bonchan, 47; BSPollard, 57; CandiceDawn, 47; yujie chen, 55; chengyuzheng, 79; ChiccoDodiFC, 12; Comstock Images, 66; Costas_Gkanasos_Photography, 53; DenKuvaiev, 79; Dimijana, 21; DmitriyKazitsyn, 85; Dmytro Diedov, 17; domonite, 34; drogatnev, 28; eag1e, 26, 77; EkaterinaZakharova, 93; Esben_H, 57; EstuaryPig, 39; ETIENJones, 49; etienne voss, 81; Evgeniya Evdokimova, 82; firina, 8; Björn Forenius, 45; fotokostic, 37; francois_t, 46; freebilly, 21; Freila, 65; gabort71, 43; Galyna0404, 63; GillTeeShots, 93; Goldi59, 15; goodmoments, 37; Grahamphoto23, 22, 23; Olga Guchek, 75; HaiMinhDuong, 30; Martin Hambleton, 31; Steve Hamilton, 75; Susan Hanko, 93; Heavily Meditated Life, 70; hekakoskinen, 38; HEMARAT, 89; HildaWeges, 8; IPGGutenbergUKLtd, 78; istetiana, 15; jatrax, 61; Jevtic, 10; Charlie Jim, 94; JPrescott, 55; Jupiterimages, 33, 48; KangeStudio, 32; KateLeigh, 17; kojihirano, 20; kynny, 47; La_vanda, 71; LeManna, 6; lensItsSelf, 13; LightFieldStudios, 90; lilu_foto, 70; Liudmyla Liudmyla, 25; lnzyx, 41; LoveTheWind, 19; Bartosz Luczak, 52; marieclaudelemay, 35; mars58, 56; maximkabb, 67; mayomtong, 9; Ryan McVay, 24; Leila Melhado, 73; MichellePatrickPhotographyLLC, 11; mirror-images, 65; mmg1design, 88; MonaMakela, 11; Monkey Business Images, 5; monstArrr_, 7; Svetlana Monyakova, 54; More86, 51; MrsWilkins, 81; nilapictures, 41; Niran_pr, 74; Ocskaymark, 97; Viktoriia Oleinichenko, 16; palinchakjr, 41; Himanshu Pandya, 64; PavelRodimov, 42, 77; phanasitti, 69; Jatuphot Phuatawee, 64; Luc Pouliot, 20; Radomir54, 52; redstallion, 68; romiri, 59; RomoloTavani, 26; Sabinoparente, 50; sgtphoto, 87; showcake, 39; Yurii Sliusar, 91; sonsam, 60; sorsillo, 72; Ssvyat, 92; Nigel Stripe, 25; SVPhilon, 81; sweetsake, 69; taratata, 56; Yana Tatevosian, 5, 58; Jennifer J Taylor, 27; Viktoriya Telminova, 46; threeart, 24; Irina_Timokhina, 63; TommyIX, 68; travnikovstudio, 4; Tuned_In, 36; v_zaitsev, 60; Vaivirga, 51; vavlt, 67; Veni vidi... shoot, 25; ViktorCap, 44; Susan Vineyard, 27; vpod, 7; vsurkov, 34; Winai_Tepsuttinun, 80; worklater1, 39; Worledit, 31; Yobro10, 33; YuriyS, 74; Zaikina, 46; Jun Zhang, 96; zocchi2, 11; Zoonar RF, 38.

We acknowledge the financial support of the Government of Canada.
Nous reconnaissons l'appui financier du gouvernement du Canada.

Funded by the Government of Canada | Canadä
Financé par le gouvernement du Canada

PC: 38-1